A Viking Easy-to-Read

MY PONY JACK

★ AT ★

Riding Lessons

By CARI MEISTER

Illustrated by AMY YOUNG

VIKING

To Aaron—C. M.

For Jack Reichardt—A. Y.

VIKING

Published by Penguin Group

Penguin Young Readers Group, 345 Hudson Street, New York, New York 10014, U.S.A.

Penguin Books Ltd, Registered Offices: 80 Strand, London WC2R 0RL, England

First published in 2005 by Viking, a division of Penguin Young Readers Group

1 3 5 7 9 10 8 6 4 2

Text copyright © Cari Meister, 2005
Illustrations copyright © Amy Young, 2005

LIBRARY OF CONGRESS CATALOGING-IN-PUBLICATION DATA
Meister, Cari.
My pony Jack at riding lessons / by Cari Meister ; illustrated by Amy Young.
p. cm.
Summary: Lacy's riding lesson with Annie, her trainer,
begins with getting the tack and ends with brushing her pony, Jack.
ISBN 0-670-05918-8 (hardcover)
[1. Horsemanship—Fiction. 2. Ponies—Fiction. 3. Stories in rhyme.]
I. Young, Amy, ill. II. Title.
PZ8.3.M5514Mya 2005   [E]—dc22   2005000779

Manufactured in China
Set in Bookman

Viking® and Easy-to-Read® are registered trademarks of Penguin Group.

Reading Level 1.8

This is my pony.

His name is Jack.

It is lesson time.

I will get the tack.

The tack room is full.

There are all kinds of things,

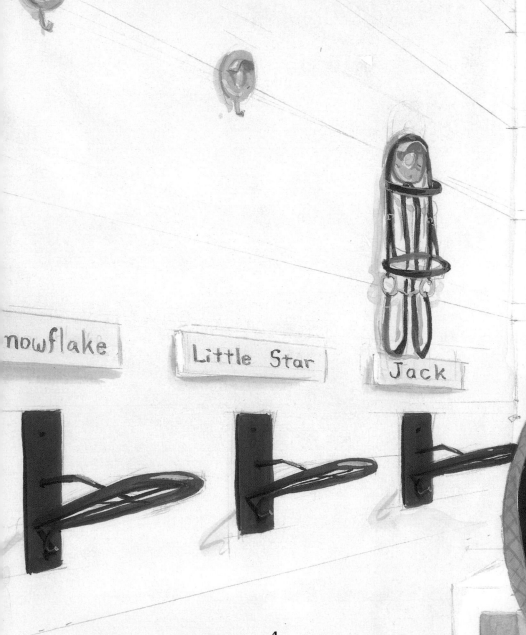

nowflake

Little Star

Jack

4

saddles and bridles,

reins and bit rings.

Jack is all set.

Now we can go.

We walk to the ring.

Easy Jack, whoa!

"Your turn, Lacy.

Your friends are ready.

"Get on Jack now.

I will hold him steady."

My trainer is Annie.

I love her big grin.

She trains me to show.

She helps me to win.

First we all walk.

"Now, everyone trot!

"Heads up. Heels down.

Watch out for that spot!"

We think it is funny.

Annie does not.

"Back to the rail, girls.
Please sit the trot."

This part is bumpy.

We hold on real tight.

"Now girls," says Annie,

"canter to the right."

I love to canter!

I am the fastest ever!

No one can catch me.

I could run forever!

"Walk now," says Annie.

"Good job for today.

Cool down your ponies,
then give them some hay."

We brush down our ponies.
Annie takes our tack.

Jack nuzzles my face.

"I love you, too, Jack!"

• PONY WORDS •

BIT RING: loop that attaches bit to bridle (the bit goes in the pony's mouth).

BRIDLE: part of the pony's tack that goes around its head; used by the rider to steer.

CANTER: a three-beat gait that is slower than a gallop (a gallop is the fastest a pony can run).

POST: the rider moves up and down in the saddle along with the pony's trot.

REINS: straps used by the rider to control the pony.

SADDLE: part of the pony's tack that goes on its back; where the rider sits.

SITTING TROT: the rider does not move up and down in the saddle, but stays "sitting."

TACK: term for all of the pony's gear including the saddle, reins, bit, and more.

TROT: a two-beat gait that is slower than a canter.

DATE DUE

DEC - 3 2005	MAY 1 6 2009
	JUL ⁀ 7 ⁀⁀⁀⁀
MAY - 4 2006	
JUN - 7 2006	SEP 0 5 2009
	AUG 0 5 2010
JUL 5 2006	AUG 2 6 2010
JUL 2 4 2006	SEP 1 4 2010
AUG 2 6 2006	
SEP 1 1 2006	JUN 0 6 2011
NOV 1 8 2006	JUL 0 7 2011
	JUL 2 6 2011
MAR 2 1 2007	APR 1 2 2014
APR 2 3 2007	MAY 2 3 2014
AUG 2 2 2007	AUG 0 2 2014
JUL 1 4 2008	NOV 2 9 2014
JUL 3 0 2008	
OCT 1 4 2008	
NOV 0 1 2008	
NOV 0 7 2008 GAYLORD	PRINTED IN U.S.A.